The School Secretary
from the
Black Lagoon

by Mike Thaler · pictures by Jared Lee

PINK
SLIP →

SCHOLASTIC INC.

New York   Toronto   London   Auckland   Sydney
Mexico City   New Delhi   Hong Kong   Buenos Aires

To Diny Gumper and all the deskateers
—M.T.

To Rosie VanDeGrift
—J.L.

ISBN 0-439-80077-3

Text copyright © 2006 by Mike Thaler.
Illustrations copyright © 2006 by Jared D. Lee Studio, Inc.

12 11 10 9 8 7   7 8 9 10 11/0

Printed in the U.S.A.
First printing, February 2006

Today my mom dropped me off late at school.

I have to go to the office and get a late slip.

I need to see Mrs. Armbender, the school secretary.

I'm scared!

I heard that she hangs you up by your thumbs
for every minute you're late.

When some kids come out of her office, their thumbs are so long they can hitchhike to Mars.

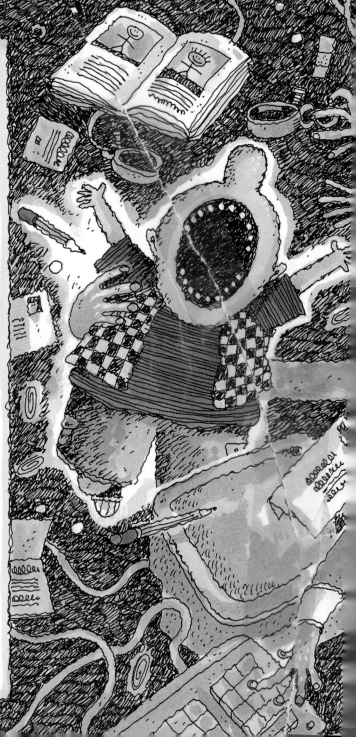

And forget about excuses.

She's heard them *all*.

She'll just string you up with two of her eight arms, while the other six are sending e-mails, sorting letters, stacking forms, signing slips, sticking on bandages, and scheduling conferences.

She must spend a fortune on underarm deodorant!

They say she runs the whole school.

You have to see her for everything!

If you're late,

If you're sick,

If you run too quick,

TRIP!

BOO HOO

I LOST MY LUNCH MONEY!

CAFETERIA

If you fall,

If you bawl,

If you shout in the hall,

If you've lost your hat,

If you find a cat,

If you need to phone

or go home,

If you miss the bus,

If you fight or fuss,

 You get sent to her.

She's all three branches of the government.

She's Congress, the Supreme Court, and the President.

 She's the power behind the throne; the voice behind the phone;

and the loudspeaker squeaker!

She's the judge and the jury—the sound and the fury.

She's Santa Claus, Frankenstein, and the Wizard of Oz—all rolled into one.

She knows everything that ever happened, is happening, or will happen at our school.

 She keeps track of every pencil, pen, and paper clip.

She even knows what you ate for breakfast.

Teachers tiptoe around her, and the principal shakes.

Well, here I am at the main office.

I go in. . . .

There's just a little lady with a pencil in her hair.

She has only two arms, but she's juggling a phone, three pink slips,

a computer mouse, and a cup of coffee.

"What can I do for you, Hubie?" she asks.

"Well, I was a few minutes late today," I mumble.

"Ten," she says, looking at her watch.

"We got stuck in traffic," I reply.

"I know," she says, "they're repairing Third Street this week.

Tell your mom to use Fifth Street instead.

And tomorrow finish your oatmeal. Today you left half of it on your face. Now run along to class."

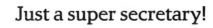

WOW!

AWESOME!

Wow! She's not so scary!

Just a super secretary!

She is message central, the Houston Space Center, and the C. I. A.
They don't call it the *main* office for nothing.

She's got radar, sonar, and *kid*-ar.

She can see through walls and down long halls.

So don't try to fool'er.

She's the ultimate ruler.

Nothing moves in or out of our school without her permission.

Even the wind needs a visitor's pass.